# The Things People Don't Say

Stella Meier

# The Things People Don't Say

Olympia Publishers
*London*

www.olympiapublishers.com
OLYMPIA PAPERBACK EDITION

Copyright © Stella Meier 2024

The right of Stella Meier to be identified as author of
this work has been asserted in accordance with sections 77 and 78 of
the Copyright, Designs and Patents Act 1988.

**All Rights Reserved**

No reproduction, copy or transmission of this publication
may be made without written permission.
No paragraph of this publication may be reproduced,
copied or transmitted save with the written permission of the publisher,
or in accordance with the provisions
of the Copyright Act 1956 (as amended).

Any person who commits any unauthorized act in relation to
this publication may be liable to criminal
prosecution and civil claims for damage.

A CIP catalogue record for this title is
available from the British Library.

ISBN: 978-1-80439-918-7

This is a work of fiction.
Names, characters, places and incidents originate from the writer's
imagination. Any resemblance to actual persons, living or dead, is
purely coincidental.

First Published in 2024

Olympia Publishers
Tallis House
2 Tallis Street
London
EC4Y 0AB

Printed in Great Britain

# Dedication

To sixteen-year-old me. You did it.

# January

January 16

A girl from my history class jumped off the roof of the science center last night. They found her body early this morning, I guess, a janitor or somebody did. Elise texted me. She said that it was pretty grotesque, that her bones were broken and her neck snapped. I got the email right after I got the text. They canceled class; Elise says it's 'cause they had to scrub the cement in order to get the blood off.

I saw it when I was walking to lunch. They had the whole area sectioned off with police tape and everything. I suppose it makes sense they used police tape, given the fact that the actual police were there. I'm not sure why they needed the cops there, she's already dead. And it's not like they have to find her murderer or anything. She left a note at least, Elise says she did. I don't know how Elise is finding all this out.

Lunch was weirdly somber. Like, everyone was too scared to talk, or if they did talk, they were talking about the dead girl and didn't want to be rude. Is it less rude to talk about her if you do it quietly?

They didn't say why they canceled class in the email, I wonder if everyone knows. I don't know how you couldn't know; everyone I see is talking about it. But, I guess I wouldn't know if Elise hadn't told me. Should I be glad she told me? At least that way I know what's going on. And shouldn't I know? I mean she's in my class and everything.

I didn't really know what to do with myself today, because

I didn't have class. I had all my homework done and stuff for class today, and I assume we're just going to do tomorrow what we were supposed to do today. I guess I could just do my homework for the rest of the week, but then I'd have to go to the library and sit through that weird not-silence again. I'd rather just stay home. Maybe Elise will invite me to dinner tonight so I won't have to eat in the cafeteria tonight.

I don't know if I really want to see Elise though. 'Cause all she's gonna talk about is the dead girl. But at least if it's with Elise, I won't have to talk back or anything. She talks enough for the both of us.

Oh, Elise just texted me.

She wants to get pizza.

January 17

They sent an email at 6:42 this morning. Classes are canceled again today. They didn't say why either. None of the campus social medias say anything about it, but the blood stain is still on the cement outside the science building. I went back to sleep after I got the email. I still don't have anything to do.

I don't remember the dead girl's name.

I suppose that's a little messed up? She was in my history class, she sat next to me, and, sometimes, we'd talk if we had to have partner discussions about things. Sometimes, she would be in the library at the same time as me. She was nice enough, I think, but I never talked to her. I wouldn't be thinking about her now if she wasn't dead.

How messed up is it to learn someone's name after they're already dead?

January 18

They sent out an official email today.

"Classes are canceled for the rest of the week, to give students and faculty an opportunity to mourn." So there's that, I guess. There's a funeral on Friday. Her name was Julia. They put a little bio at the bottom of the email. I guess her name wasn't even important enough to put at the top of the email about her funeral. She had a cat.

Elise sent me a screenshot of the school's hashtag. She says it's blowing up. Everyone's posting about her. But I don't think she had very many friends. She never met anybody after class, and Elise always waited for me after history. And when I saw her in the library, she was always by herself. Everyone's posting about her though. You'd think she was friends with the whole school.

All the professors are putting out statements of how sorry they are and how we are supposed to take this time for our mental health. Whatever that means. My history professor hasn't put anything out yet though, I wonder if he forgot she was in his class.

I went to the cafeteria for lunch, (I was hungry enough to deal with the not-silence) and the counseling center set up shop in the entryway.

The head counselor stopped me when I walked in.

"This is such a difficult time for all of us, have you been

taking care of yourself?" she asked.

"Why do I need to take care of myself?"

"Suicide impacts the whole community. It can lead to a domino effect and we really want to prevent that from happening."

The head counselor is kind of a funny-looking woman. She's really tall and skinny and reminds me of a stick bug.

"Did you know her?"

She gave me a pamphlet about self-harm.

When I sat down next to Elise, she showed me her pamphlet. It was about teenage suicide. But Elise isn't a teenager. She's 20.

"They've been stopping everybody. They must've given out a thousand pamphlets by now. Mostly just stuff about different types of suicide and how to tell if someone's going to kill themselves or not. If you ask me, it's all a little too late. It's not going to save that girl, she's already dead."

I watched her take a bite of her burger. The cafeteria was kinda empty. I guess a lot of people lost their appetite after learning how to commit suicide.

January 19

They've set up a memorial for Julia in the science center. Elise and I went for a walk around campus today, because I was tired of watching TV and she was apparently tired of painting her nails. (One hand is blue and the other is green) (I didn't say anything about it, because I can't tell if she did it on purpose or not).

But anyway, they set up a memorial in the science center. There's a huge life-size photograph of her; I think they used her senior photo; she's in that generic sunflower field they use for senior photos. She looks happy enough in the photo, I guess. They also displayed what amounted to her accomplishments. Her high school diploma, an unfinished painting from her art class, a photo of her cat. A book she was in the middle of reading. And her suicide note.

It was a letter to her little brother.

I read part of it, but I stopped reading halfway through. After she told him that no matter what people said, she still loved him.

If I killed myself, I don't think I'd want the whole school reading my suicide note.

And if I was her little brother, I think I'd wonder how she loved me but not enough to stay.

January 21

Sorry, I'm writing this a bit late. Although I guess it doesn't really matter. But I haven't had time to write since the funeral.

Elise came over yesterday morning to help me get ready. The funeral started at two, and she came at eleven and she brought McDonald's, so it wasn't so bad. I had to borrow a dress from her because I don't own any black dresses. She curled my hair for me, which was nice. I think if I killed myself, I'd miss Elise curling my hair.

Elise talked the whole time we got ready. She saw a duck on the side of the road on her way to my dorm. The line at McDonald's was very short. She found 3 dollars on the sidewalk yesterday. The college's Facebook page gained 700 followers over the week. (Apparently, suicide is a lucrative social media gain). I think this whole thing is affecting Elise more than me. Elise talks a lot on a normal day, but when she's nervous, she talks even more.

"Is everything okay?"

Her hands were really cold when she brushed my neck, fluffing out my hair.

"Yeah, of course." Her smile was kinda watery though. "It's just. You'd—you'd tell me, right?"

"Tell you what?"

"If you were gonna do something like that."

"You mean like jump off the building."

She flinched.

"Don't say it like that. But yeah."

"I think telling you about it would sorta defeat the purpose."

"Jesus, I'm serious."

"I am too. If I would tell you, you'd try to stop me. So, I probably wouldn't."

"Yeah, okay whatever."

She was mad, which I probably deserved. I knew what she meant. I turned around in my chair and really looked at her.

"I'm sorry."

"It's fine."

"No, I mean it. I'm sorry. I'd tell you. Who else would I tell?"

She smiled at me. A real smile.

I think if I killed myself, I'd miss her smile too.

Elise and I walked to the funeral together. I guess that's pretty self-explanatory though. And also, I mean, we didn't have to go to the funeral. But everyone was invited. We didn't talk about not going.

They held it in the arena. There were a lot of people there. Like probably a thousand. And everyone was packed into the arena, shoulder to shoulder. It was horrendous. I don't think even half those people had even seen her before.

The president of the university came to kick things off. That was probably a bad way to phrase it, but that's what he did. He gave a little speech about how sad everything was, how help is available to those who need it, and how the college was going to miss her. What a joke.

Then Julia's mom came. She could hardly talk, she was crying so hard. But her speech was mostly about how glad she was that her daughter had such great friends and such a great place to go to school. I sorta got the feeling her mom didn't really know much of what her daughter's life was like.

Then they played a little video about her life. Pictures of her when she was a baby to pictures of her two weeks ago, before she was dead. The video made Elise really sad, she started tearing up when Julia's mom came out, but she started really crying during the video.

I saw the kid who must've been Julia's brother sitting next to the mom and the president in the front row. He was wearing a suit that didn't really fit him, the cuffs were way too long and they dragged on the floor. He wasn't crying. He wasn't doing much of anything really. I don't think he was listening. But I wasn't really either. I wonder if he knew that everyone at the university had read the goodbye letter his sister had written him.

After the video, the brother and the mom stood behind the president and walked from the front podium all the way to the back doors. The brother was carrying a little pot which must've been Julia's ashes. He wasn't really watching where he was going and I got really worried that he was going to trip over his too-long pants and fall in front of everyone. After they left, people started filing out. The students weren't invited to the graveyard. I'm not sure where they took the ashes. They didn't tell us, but we weren't invited. Elise and I went back to my dorm. It was cold outside, but my winter coat is black so it's all right. Elise forgot her gloves, so I gave her mind, because I walk with my hands in my pockets anyway.

When we got back to the dorm, Elise didn't change or anything, she just got in my bed, and gestured to me. It was only 5 and I wasn't tired, but I went anyway.

When I got into bed, Elise didn't say anything for a really long time. She just looked at me, in that weird way she does sometimes.

"What did you think?"

"About what?"

"The funeral."

"Oh." I didn't really know what I thought. I didn't really know what I thought about this whole thing. "I guess. I thought it was weird that everyone in the school was there. You know, most of those people didn't know her."

"We didn't know her."

"I know."

"You didn't know her brother either, but you still cared about him."

"It's not that I cared about him. I just didn't want him to fall in front of everybody. You know. He was carrying his sister's ashes. And everybody knows what she wrote to him in her letter."

"That's caring."

"It's not. I didn't know them."

She didn't say anything for a long while. I started to drift off, even though it was still early and I still wasn't tired. It was just comfortable in bed with Elise. I had the passing thought that there really wasn't anywhere I'd rather be. If I kill myself, I'd miss that.

When I woke up this morning, she had already left. She texted me and said that she'd had an appointment to get to, but I think she just needed to think about things for a while. That's okay, you know. She didn't have to lie about it or anything.

I went to the cafeteria for lunch by myself. It was pretty empty like it usually is on Saturdays. But on all the TVs, instead of the campus news page, they had Julia's memorial page. It was pretty morbid which the cafeteria usually isn't on Saturdays.

January 22

Elise came over this afternoon and we went for a walk. She seemed like she was feeling better.

January 23

Classes resumed today. I was behind in my history class, because the professor had assumed we were going to keep up with our homework. One of the kids who sat in the front row got into an argument about it.

"The emails said we didn't have to do any homework over the mourning week. We were supposed to use it, to like mourn and stuff."

"I'm sorry if you used your break to be lazy, but that's not my problem. The syllabus includes the dates and times that the assignments are due and it's your responsibility to keep up with them."

"It wasn't a break, Professor. A girl died."

"I'm not going to allow you to use another classmate as an excuse."

But he ended up extending everything another week anyway, so I guess he didn't really mean it. But that still means we had double the homework we were supposed to have and I was supposed to go to a movie with Elise tonight. And I guess I'm procrastinating doing the homework 'cause I'm writing this instead, but I don't really like history homework. I don't really like that class, either. And anyway, I'm supposed to go to a movie with Elise later, so I won't finish anyway.

The movie was really good.

Elise and I sat in the way back and made fun of all the bad

acting. It was a low-budget rom-com, which I hate, but it was really fun. She stuck her hand in my pocket on the way back 'cause she forgot her gloves again. I told her I didn't mind if she borrowed mine, but she said it was warmer in my pockets than in the gloves.

January 26

Hey, sorry, I'm writing this really rushed because I have to leave in 10 minutes to go to dinner with my dad. He's freaking because I guess I forgot to tell him that Julia killed herself. Apparently when something big happens like that, I'm supposed to tell him. Anyway.

The college set up this, like, mental health booster clinic thing in the student lounge. And the, like, idea is to make it super easy for students to talk about their mental health and get help if they need it, but all they had there were coloring pages and the suicide hotline phone number. So, I guess mental health doesn't exist unless you're about to kill yourself.

It's later now. I went to dinner with my dad, and like I don't really write about my dad that much, but it's 'cause we don't really see each other much. My dad doesn't really get out much, he's one of those people who think everything is out to get him, germs, the government, society in general, you know. He used to make me wear a mask out in public when I was little so I wouldn't get sick.

"I wish you would've called me." We both got spaghetti. It was a fancy Italian place, well fancy for us.

"I know. I'm sorry, I just didn't think you'd hear about it, I guess."

"That's my point. Just 'cause you didn't think I'd hear about it doesn't mean you shouldn't tell me."

"That's not what I meant, you know, I just didn't want you to worry about me."

"I always worry about you."

"Well, it's not like suicide's contagious or anything."

We ate in silence for a while. The Italian place gives us this free bread with our meals and I ate three pieces and my dad ate one. I felt kinda bad and I asked him if he wanted to split it but he said no.

"My history professor said we have to make up all the work for the week they canceled class. Which is totally unfair, 'cause now I have twice as much homework this week."

"I don't think it's very polite to say that having homework is unfair after what happened to that poor girl."

"That's not what I mean, Dad. And I guess it's like not proportional or anything, but still."

"I know." He picked at his bread. "I read in the newspaper that all that poor girl had was her mother and her little brother. Her dad died from skin cancer."

"That sucks."

"They call it the silent killer, you know?"

"I'm pretty sure they don't call it that."

"It's just so sad. That poor girl."

I think if I killed myself, I'd hate it if people would call me 'that poor girl.' She made the decision, you know. It's not something that happened to her. It's something she did. Or maybe that's too harsh. I don't know what she wants to be called, and I guess that poor girl is better than that dead girl.

January 27

We had a group discussion in history today. Julie was always my partner before. Whenever we had to do a discussion. I guess I didn't realize or what, but when the professor said to get into discussion groups, I turned like she was going to be sitting right behind me. But she wasn't. She's dead now. I don't think it really hit me before. But it did then. Julie couldn't be my partner anymore just like she couldn't do anything anymore. She wouldn't sit behind me in class and be in my group and laugh at my stupid comments about the professor. She wouldn't sit two tables diagonal from me in the library. She wouldn't wave at me when she saw me in the hallway. She couldn't do any of that anymore because she was dead.

    The professor put me in another group.

January 30

We spent the whole weekend at Elise's house. Her parents went on some vacation – I think she said to Mexico – and she didn't want to be alone so she invited me. I didn't mind. Her mom always leaves her a credit card so Elise can get snacks because all her mom eats is that weird protein stuff. We went to the store Friday night and bought like $100 of food, and then we still ended up ordering takeout for every meal. Elise said her mom wouldn't even notice, which I think is true. Elise's mom doesn't notice a lot. I honestly don't think she even knows we're friends.

Friday night, we just stayed in and broke into Elise's parents' liquor cabinet. Which isn't really anything fancy. It's just the cabinet over the fridge that Elise's parents think she doesn't know about. Or maybe they know she knows and they just don't care. We never replace anything.

She made these mixers with lemonade and we did manicures. Elise does mine and I do hers. I always feel bad because she's so much better at it than me and mine always looks better 'cause whenever I start to paint her nails, my hands start to shake. She says she doesn't mind though. We always take photos for her Instagram. I'm featured on Elise's Instagram more than she is, I think. We got pizza and Elise filled me in on all the gossip I missed. Which was a lot! I filled Elise in on the fact that my neighbor has a pet rat.

Saturday, we went to the mall. I love the mall. But it's more fun when I go with Elise. We went to every single store at least once and tried what felt like everything on. Elise bought me a necklace with my zodiac sign on it. I bought her a hat. She said she's never taking it off. So I said I wasn't either.

Last night, we watched a movie. I don't remember which movie it was because Elise and I talked the whole way through it. She fixed the spots on my nails that I smudged, and I ate ice cream.

"What do you think the meaning of life is?"

"I don't know," I said around a spoonful of ice cream. "This, probably."

"Ugh, I'm serious."

"So am I!"

She rolled her eyes at me, but I really was serious.

"Being with you is the meaning of life for me. That's why I'm here."

She looked at me for a long time. She does that a lot. Always gives me these long looks.

"You're such a sap, you know that?"

"Yeah, whatever. What's it for you then?"

"Are you sure there is one?"

"What do you mean?"

"I don't know. I guess just sometimes, it feels like there really isn't a meaning to any of it. Like, we just wake up every day and then one day we die."

"Maybe," I said. "But at least I get to wake up next to you."

She threw a pillow at my face.

"Why do you ask?" I said.

"Ask what?"

"Oh my god, you weirdo, about the meaning of life."

"Oh, I don't know. I've just been thinking about it a lot lately."

"Don't think too hard. You'll hurt yourself."

"You suck."

# February

February 3

They took down the mental health center in the student lounge. They replaced it with a free concert ticket giveaway. Some B-list celebrity is coming to perform on campus for Valentine's Day. But I don't care, mostly because I don't know who it is, but also because Elise and I already have plans for Valentine's Day. We're going to the mall to buy chocolate and then going back to my dorm to watch terrible movies. It's what we always do on Valentine's Day.

February 4

Elise and I got into a fight today. It was awful. We never fight. It's part of why we're such good friends. Elise lets me be right about dumb stuff and I let her be right about stuff that's important. It's a nice thing we have going on. We met at the cafeteria for lunch at noon like we always do, but I was a couple minutes late. Usually, I'm a couple minutes early and Elise is the one a couple minutes late, so I didn't think it would be that big of a deal.

"You're late."

It was a big deal.

"Just a couple minutes."

"Yeah well, I was waiting for you, you made me look stupid."

"Oh, I'm sorry. It's just, usually, you're a few minutes late, so I didn't realize you were waiting."

"Oh right. So, it's my fault."

Elise was being weird. She's never really like that. She must not have gotten enough sleep last night.

"It's not anybody's fault? I was just a couple minutes late, it's not a big deal."

"You don't get to tell me what's a big deal and what's not a big deal. You said you'd be here at twelve and you weren't. You lied."

"Did you talk to your mom today?"

"Jesus Christ. I'm done with this."

And she left.

In hindsight, it was kind of a dick move to bring up her mom like that, but I really just meant it as, like, Elise is always frustrated after she talks to her mom 'cause her mom is kind of the worst. Like she never asks Elise how she is or anything, and she always brings up Elise applying to law school. Elise does not want to go to law school. But anyway, it was kind of rude asking that but I just meant it as, like, a question.

I texted her, at suppertime, to see if she wanted to get supper because she never ate anything for lunch. But she didn't respond until nine and then she said she wasn't hungry.

I hate when Elise is mad at me. I always get this horrible feeling in my stomach like I'm gonna die or something. Maybe I'll bring her a coffee in the morning.

February 5


I brought Elise a coffee this morning.
 "Oh, what's this for?"
 "I felt bad about what I said yesterday. I didn't mean it."
 "What?"
 "I'm sorry I was late."
 "What are you talking about? There's nothing to be sorry for. Thanks for the coffee."

February 8

It was so warm today! The sun was shining, the snow was melting, and I didn't even wear a coat this morning. Elise and I walked to the park after class; she packed a little blanket that we laid out. It was so nice. I brought a book to read and Elise braided my hair. After a while, we just kinda lay there and watched the clouds go by. It was the best day.

"That one looks like a bird."

"They all look like birds; you're not trying very hard."

I made a face at her. "Fine, that one looks like a big, fluffy cloud."

She tugged on the end of my hair and stuck her tongue out. "I think that one looks like a dragon."

"Yeah, maybe a wimpy dragon. Oh! That one looks like a tree."

"What kinda tree?"

"Hmm, like a big willow tree."

"It does not!"

"It so does."

February 9

The counseling center is doing a suicide prevention course. I was thinking maybe I would do it, you know, because of everything, but when I mentioned it to Elise, she got really weird about it.
"Why would you want to do that?"
"I don't know. In case."
"In case of what?"
"Well, in case somebody I know is gonna do it."
"Are you going to?"
"Go to the class?"
"No, commit suicide."
"No?"
"Then you don't need to take the course."
Even though she said I didn't need to, I was still really thinking about it. The flyer said that it could help save lives or whatever. I called my dad to see what he said about it.
"You're gonna do what?"
"Are you even listening to me?"
"Yes, sorry, I was disinfecting the living room."
"Don't you have work today? Why are you at home?"
"I wasn't feeling well this morning, so I stayed home."
"Oh, geez, Dad, did you go to the doctor?"
"No, doctors will kill you. I'm sure I have the flu."
"Do you have a fever?"
"Yes."

"What is it?"

"I don't know, the thermometer isn't working."

"What's wrong with the thermometer?"

"It was saying my temperature was 98, but I know I have a fever."

"Oh."

"Anyway, why are you calling?"

"Oh, right. They're doing this suicide prevention course at school, 'cause of everything that happened with that girl, and I was thinking of going to it."

"Hm, why?"

"Well, so I could recognize the signs, or whatever, you know, so I could help someone."

"And you're telling me this because?"

"Do you think I should go?"

"I don't know. I mean it can't really be that useful, right? 'Cause all those counselors didn't even notice when it was that poor girl, and they're certified. Do you really think you could do anything when they couldn't?"

"I mean, I guess not. Elise didn't think I should do it either."

"She's a smart girl. How is she doing, by the way?"

"She's fine. Good."

"That's good. Tell her I said hi, will you?"

"Yeah."

"Oh, honey, I have to go, I need to take my next dose of medicine."

"All right. I'll talk to you later."

February 13

Elise missed class this morning, which is, I realize, not that big of a deal, but Elise never misses class. Like ever. I skipped once during our freshman year, and she gave me a twenty-minute lecture about how much money I was wasting. So, I don't miss class. Besides, Elise always waits for me after my morning class, and she usually brings me a snack. But today, she wasn't there which is how I know she skipped class. I called her on my way to my second class.

"Hey."

"You missed class this morning."

"I know, I'm sorry, I was going to text you not to wait for me, but I forgot."

"Are you okay?"

"Yeah, why do you ask?"

"You never miss class. You say it's a waste of money."

"It is. But my alarm didn't go off this morning, and I was so tired."

I got the feeling Elise was lying to me. As long as I've known her, she's set like three alarms every morning because she hates being late.

"Oh."

"I'm all right, promise. I'll see you at lunch, okay?"

February 15

Good morning. Or afternoon, I guess. It's 12:03, so afternoon. I'm writing this while Elise is in the shower, 'cause when she's done, we're going to get breakfast. Or, lunch.

Yesterday was Valentine's Day. Obviously, but yeah.

They set up the campus green with cutesy little Valentine's decorations and a little stage for the singer. Everywhere you looked, it looked like a hallmark store threw up on it. I love Valentine's Day.

Elise and I went to the mall in the afternoon after classes. We hit up the perfume store and I bought Elise a Valentine's Day themed one. Then we went to the Hallmark store and tried on Valentine's Day headbands and took a picture for Elise's Instagram. Then we went to the chocolate store, which is my favorite. We always buy like 10 pounds of chocolate.

We went to Elise's because her parents were out – they went to a dinner party and Elise said they wouldn't be home 'til the weekend. We made pizza and drank champagne and watched *The Shining*. And then I ate so much chocolate that I threw up. It was the best.

February 16

Today is the one-month anniversary of the day Julia jumped off the science center. I didn't realize it until Elise and I went to lunch and they had the memorial video on the TV screens again. Nobody really noticed, I don't think. It was super loud in the cafeteria. I wouldn't have noticed if it wasn't for Elise. She stared at it for a long time.

February 17

They took down Julia's shrine in the science center. They replaced it with a thing about climate change.

February 20

I am exhausted. I mean it was really my own fault, but I'm still grumpy about it. Elise called me last night at 2, and obviously, I was sleeping but she's usually in bed long before I am so I answered the phone.
"Jesus, do you know what time it is?"
"Um, no, not really."
"It's 2 o'clock in the morning, are you okay?"
"Yeah, no, I'm okay, sorry. I just… couldn't sleep."
"You couldn't sleep?"
"Yeah, I don't know. I must've had like a weird dream or something, but I woke up and couldn't fall back asleep."
"So, you decided to wake me up because you were?"
"… Yeah. Is that bad?"
"No, it's fine."
We ended up talking until like 5, and then when she finally fell asleep, my goddamn alarm went off. So, here I am. Exhausted. She skipped class again, which I mean I get, 'cause she didn't sleep all night.

February 21

Elise didn't text me back one time today. She skipped class again (2 days in a row).

February 22

Elise brought me a muffin today when she met me after class. I think she felt bad about waking me up the other night, but I told her like a hundred times that it was fine. She was in a really good mood today and she ended up coming over to my dorm after classes to play Mario Kart.

February 24


Elise has been really tired this last week so we went to get manicures today. I'm not sure how that's supposed to help her be less tired, but it was her idea. My idea was taking a nap. Our nails turned out pretty though, so we took a photo for Elise's Instagram.

After we got our nails done, we ate supper at the food court in the mall. I love the food court. I got pizza and Elise got tacos, but we ended up switching because tacos sounded really good to me and Elise wasn't very hungry so she just wanted a few bites of pizza.

"Do you ever think about what you're going to do after school?"

I frowned at her for interrupting my tacos.

"Well, I mean, yeah, all the time. Why don't you?"

"Of course I do, weirdo, I brought it up."

"Okay then, what's your point?"

"Well, it's just like, I know we talked about moving to the cities after graduation."

"Yeah?"

"Do you ever think about going before?"

"Like on spring break?"

"No, dumbass, like now."

"But I have school."

"Drop out."

"What?"

"Drop out of school. We could go wherever we wanted. We could move to Greece or something and live on the beach."

"You want to drop out of school? What about like money and our futures?"

"Don't worry about money, I have my trust fund, I'll pay for everything."

"How would that even work, where would we live, what would we do?"

"We'd be together!" She grabbed my hand and got this really intense look in her eye. "I thought you said I was your life."

"You are. It's just, I like school and I want to get my degree and then maybe after we could go to Greece?"

"You don't get it."

"I'm not saying no!"

"Don't you feel trapped here?"

"No, I don't! Do you?"

"Yes! That's the point. This place is suffocating. I thought you'd understand."

February 25

I went home this weekend. Mostly 'cause Elise's parents were home so she couldn't hang out. My dad and I met for lunch this afternoon and then afterward we went home. Tomorrow, we have plans to go to a movie. It's one Elise and I already saw but my dad was excited about it, so I didn't tell him.

"So how are things?"

"Dad, did you bring your own silverware again? That is so weird."

"You have no idea how disgusting the restaurant's silverware is, they don't even sanitize them. I'm this close to bringing my own plate."

"Oh my god."

"Anyway, how are things?"

"Oh, I mean, they're fine. School's going fine. We're getting into the thick of things now, you know."

"Mmhmm."

"Oh! I was going to tell you, I finished my sculpture for my art class, it's a version of the Oedipus mask for traditional Greek theater."

"You know, I played Oedipus in college during Greek week."

"Yes, I know, you've told me that story like a hundred times."

"And how's your dorm? Have you been using the disinfectant spray I gave you?"

"Yes, Dad, and I'm still not sick, so you don't have to worry."

"I always worry. And how's Elise? I saw her father at the office yesterday."

"Oh, she's fine. You know how it is."

February 26

Dad and I went for a walk after the movie. It was really nice outside, and the weather has been pleasant for February. It's probably a sign of global warming or something, but my Dad and I used it as a chance to be outside.

"Are you eating enough at school?"

"Yeah, I've got the meal plan and stuff."

"No, I know. But, you're using it and everything?"

"Yeah."

"Good."

"Hey, can I ask you something?"

"Depends."

"What do you think is the meaning of life?"

"What? Why do you ask?"

"I don't know. Elise brought it up the other day, and I've just been thinking about it, I guess."

"Oh. I don't really know, I guess. I don't think about it that much."

"Why not?"

"I don't devote much time to thinking about stuff like that. I've got to worry about you."

"Oh."

February 27

Elise skipped class again. She said she was tired after dealing with her mom all weekend, but she met me for lunch.
"What the hell is that?"
"It's a tuna sandwich."
"That doesn't answer my question."
"My dad made it for me."
"Because he hates you?"
"What?"
"You hate tuna."
"He didn't have anything else. You know he worries that I go hungry."
"That doesn't mean you have to eat it."
"I'm gonna. He made it for me."

# March

March 1

Elise canceled on me today. We made plans yesterday to go roller skating. And this morning when I texted her to see if she wanted me to pick her up or if she wanted to drive, she never responded. I waited all day. I'm actually, like, mad at her. And I'm never mad at her. I don't know what to do with myself.

March 2

I didn't see Elise today at all. She didn't go to class, and she didn't show up to wait for me outside of class either. And she didn't come to lunch. I'm worried about her. It's not like her to not respond to me. We've never gone more than a day without talking before.

March 3


I'm writing this at Elise's house. She's sleeping.

I went to Elise's dorm today because I was worried she might be dead or something. I knocked on her door for 5 minutes before she finally opened it. I swear to god I was 30 seconds away from calling the police. I was talking before she even got the door open all the way.

"Where the hell have you been? I've been worried about you, asshole! You don't respond to my texts or show up to class. I thought you were dead!"

"Oh, shit. I am so sorry. I totally forgot we were supposed to go roller skating."

"Wait, what?"

"I must've slept through my alarm."

"What the hell. Elise, that was two days ago."

"What?"

"It's *Friday*. We were supposed to go roller skating on Wednesday."

"It's Friday?"

"That's it. I'm coming in."

The place was so messy. It seemed like she had been sleeping on the living room couch because the entire floor was covered in blankets, empty water bottles, and wrinkly clothes. I still don't know how she managed to get it that messy in a few days because Elise's mom always hires a cleaner before she comes back to town.

I managed to convince Elise to take a shower because her hair was, truthfully, horrifically greasy. I picked up some of the clothes off the floor and managed to find something clean in her closet. But let's face it, I'm not much of a cleaner either, so I mostly just shoved stuff aside and threw an armful of plastic water bottles into the trash and then ordered a pizza.

"Do I need to take you to the doctor?"

"What, no? I'm not sick."

"You've been sleeping for three days straight. That's not normal."

"Dude, I'm fine. I'm not going to the doctor. I've just been really tired lately."

"Have you not been taking care of yourself? Do you have too much homework or something? You've been missing a lot of classes; do you need me to help you catch up on your assignments?"

"No, I'm fine, relax. I'm just tired."

March 5

I wanted to spend the weekend at Elise's, mostly to make sure she didn't die or something while I was gone, but she said I couldn't 'cause her mom was coming to town. Her mom's been coming to town a lot lately. I think she's been there more in the last couple of weeks than she was all of last year. But at least then she'll hire a cleaner for Elise.

Elise wanted to make up for skipping out on roller skating so she said she'd take me to the mall after school tomorrow. I love the mall.

March 6

She canceled.

March 7

Elise was waiting for me after class today with Starbucks. I'm not good at being mad at her, so I told her not to worry about it. At least she went to class.

March 9

My dad sent me a blanket in the mail. He said he's worried about me being cold, even though it's been warm this winter. I was going to tell Elise about it, but I didn't want her to feel bad 'cause her parents don't do nice stuff like that. Plus, she hasn't responded to my last text from yesterday, so.

March 11

Elise invited me to go with her and her family on spring break! This is so exciting. We're going to the beach to stay at her family's beach house. We went to the mall today to get swimsuits for it, not to go swimming in, but to lie on the beach. Ah, it's going to be amazing.

March 12

My dad is very nervous about me going to the beach. He says sand has germs and the ocean is dangerous. We made a compromise that in exchange for him not freaking out, he can buy me one (1) lifejacket that I promise to take with me.

March 14

We got manicures for the beach today!

March 16

I honestly think Elise has just given up on this semester. She hasn't been to a full day of classes in forever. I think spring break will be good for her. You know, get out of town, lay in the sun for a while, and not worry about anything. Plus, you know, I'm going to have a blast. I'm gonna buy a floppy hat.

March 20

It is very early in the morning, Elise will be here soon to pick me up for break (her parents are meeting us there). I'm so excited.

    Okay, it's night now. Elise is sleeping.
    She lied to me.
    Her parents are not coming. She said they originally were going to and then canceled at the last minute and she didn't want to tell me because she was afraid my dad wouldn't let me go then. First of all, I'm a grown-up, my dad isn't the boss of me, and I can do whatever I want. And second of all, I can't believe she lied! We don't lie to each other. We just don't. And I'm not saying it's that big of a deal that her parents were here or not, the problem is that she lied about it. And I don't even know why she lied in the first place! She knows I know her parents are flakey. They do stuff like this all the time. And I guess, maybe she was mad at them for flaking, or she wanted to pretend like maybe they would come or something. I don't know. Elise does weird stuff like that sometimes. And I guess I'm not really that mad about it. I still get to go to the beach.

March 21

The beach is amazing.
    I love it here. I'm never leaving. I can see why Elise wants to move to Greece if it's like this every day. It's so warm here and we're only a few hours south. It's amazing. And the beach is pretty much deserted, because the house her parents own is right on the water. Plus, Elise says most people that live here aren't used to the cooler weather so they don't come this time of year. Which is so stupid. If I lived here, I'd go to the beach every single day. Oh! And we didn't spend all day at the beach or anything. We walked down to the center of the town which is this cute little boardwalk with all these shops. Elise and I bought matching bracelets and we got ice cream. I could live here.

March 22

We had a picnic on the beach today! I made the sandwiches and Elise got strawberries from the store. I don't know what it is, but everything tastes so much better on the beach.

"Okay, you know what. You were right about Greece. Let's drop out of college and just live on the beach. This is amazing."

"Ha, if you're that impressed with this, wait till I take you to a real beach. Maybe somewhere in the Bahamas."

"The Bahamas?"

"You're too much. Yes, the Bahamas."

"Why would you take me?"

"Who else would I go with?"

March 23

Elise and I spent the morning at this little cafe in town. We both got chocolate chip pancakes and Elise wasn't very hungry, so she let me eat hers. They were delicious. Then, of course, we spent the afternoon on the beach. I read a little bit, mostly just to stay awake, because Elise fell asleep in the sun, so I had to wake her up every couple of hours to make her put more sunscreen on and flip over so she didn't get a weird tan. We made spaghetti in her parents' kitchen for supper and ate it while we watched a rom-com. I don't remember what it was called but Matthew McConaughey was in it. Elise loves him. Then we went back out to the beach once it got dark to go night swimming. Which, oh my god, is so fun. I've never done it before, but I loved it. Elise said we should make it a tradition.

"Hey, I want you to know something."
"What's that?"
"I love you."
"Aww." I gave her a sloppy kiss on the forehead. "I love you too."
"No. I'm serious."
"I'm serious too!"
"No, just, look at me for a second."
"I want you to know that I love you. Like, you're it for me. I don't want anybody else in my life."
"What do you mean?"
"I mean, like, I don't ever want to get married. I don't care

what job I get or if I graduate college or anything. I don't want to go to law school. I don't care about any of that. All I care about is you. I'll wait 'til you graduate school and then we can go wherever you want. I'll buy you a house. We'll go to the Bahamas every year in the spring. I don't care. I'll go everywhere with you. And if you don't let me, I'll die."

"Elise, hey, why wouldn't I let you?"

"I don't know, but I mean it. If I'm not with you, I'll die."

"I want to be with you too. We can, I don't know, move to Greece and open a shop selling magic potions and spend all day on the beach."

"You mean it?"

"Yeah, of course, you're my best friend. I love you."

"But I love you more than that. You can't ever leave me. Not to get married. I'll die."

"You're not going to die. I'll never leave you."

"Promise?"

"Promise. Besides, who will I ever love more than you?"

March 25

We are leaving the beach today. I don't know how I'll ever be happy again. Just kidding. But I got the most horrific sunburn yesterday, so I can't hold a pen. Or sit. Or go to the bathroom. Or do much of anything actually. I think Elise is sadder about leaving than I am, actually. It was nice to see her so carefree these last couple of days. Maybe I can convince her to come up here more often, even if it's not with me. I think she needs more time in the sun.

March 27

My sunburn has finally healed enough for me to be able to do normal things by myself again. Just in time to go back to class. Yay. And also, I know this is weird. But like, I kinda miss Elise? Seeing her every day and spending all day with her was really nice.

March 29

I don't know what I thought would happen. Like after we spent spring break together, Elise would magically stop skipping class and canceling on me? But no, she has not. She skipped class today and said she couldn't get lunch because she was behind on homework. Which yeah, I know she's behind on homework. There's no way she's managed to keep up with everything. She never does it when we're together and when we're not together, she's sleeping! But that doesn't mean she can't get lunch with me.

March 30

Elise skipped class again. Three days in a row.

March 31

I haven't heard from Elise since Tuesday.

# April

April 2

Elise says she feels bad for not talking to me last week. Which, yeah. I don't know how she can go from being so intense about how much she loves me and wants to spend the rest of our lives together one week, but then the next week she doesn't talk to me, like at all. But anyway, she said she was going to pick me up in a bit to take me to the mall to make up for it. But I'm not going to get my hopes up because the last time she said she was going to take me to the mall, she canceled.

It's later. We went to the mall! Except now, I feel guilty about being so sure she was going to cancel. I underestimated her. I should apologize. Or no. I shouldn't. 'Cause then I'd have to tell her I thought she wasn't going to show. And that would just make her feel bad, because I know she's been struggling with being so tired lately. Maybe I should start slipping her vitamins?

April 4

Elise has gone to class two days in a row! And waited for me after class and walked to class with me! Is this love?

April 7

Yeah, lol. No. She did not go to class the rest of the week. And we can't even hang out this weekend because her stupid parents are home, again. Why are they coming home so much? They don't like being here.

April 8

I decided to go home this weekend because I couldn't hang out with Elise, but then I felt bad because how come I only go home when I can't spend the weekend with her? That's not very fair to my dad. So to make up for it, I bought him a book on fishing. He doesn't like going fishing. He just likes reading about fishing.

"So, how've you been?"
"Oh, you know. School is school."
"Yeah? Classes okay and everything?"
"Yeah. Oh, I have something for you."
"You do?"
"Mmhmm."
"It's a book!"
"About fishing."
"Oh, thank you, honey. I love it. You know, fishing is actually how your mom and I met."

I know. And I know that every time my dad hears or thinks about fishing, he brings up this story.

"Really?"
"Yeah. My college roommate thought it would be hilarious to sign me up for the fishing contest my college was hosting. You had to be in teams of two and whoever caught the largest fish in three hours won like a hundred dollars or something, I don't remember the prize."

"But you were signed up by yourself?"

"And so was your mother. So, they paired us up together. But she was so into it, your mom was. She was from a big outdoorsy family and she was determined to win, and I tried explaining to her that I didn't know how to fish and my friend had only signed me up as a prank, but they wouldn't let her do it by herself, so she told me to sit in the corner of the boat, gave me a book just like this, and told me to read out descriptions of fish to see if she could guess the name of it."

"She won it, right? The competition?"

"She sure did. The biggest fish by far. But she was so funny and told everyone it was because I was her good luck charm. She wouldn't go fishing without me after that."

April 10

Elise texted me ahead of time today to let me know she wouldn't be coming to class today. Which is like, yep, I knew. But she said she'd meet me for lunch and then didn't show up, so, you know. And also, Elise said her parents are staying at their house all week. I don't remember the last time they stayed for longer than a weekend.

April 11

Elise came to lunch today, but I think it would've been better if she just stayed home.

"He's been bringing his own silverware to work now too, even though they provide it. And I keep telling him that it's so weird and people are going to think he's insane—"

"Uh-huh."

"Hey, are you even listening to me?"

"That's cool."

"Elise?"

"Mmhmm."

"Elise!"

"Jesus, what, why are you yelling?"

"Oh good, you can hear me. I was wondering if I had forgotten to talk out loud or something."

"What?"

"You're not even listening to me."

"No, I'm listening."

"Right, what was I talking about?"

"Um…"

"Exactly."

"Well, sorry! You've been talking for like fifteen minutes and it was getting hard to listen."

"I was not—"

"Yes, you were. All you do is talk all the time, it's exhausting. I can't even hear myself think because I'm too busy listening to you tell the same story over and over again."

"Hey, why—"

"I'm not being mean, you're being annoying. I'm not hungry anymore; I'm just going to go."

April 13

"Hey, Dad."

"Oh hey, honey, what's up? Why are you calling me, is something wrong?"

"No, why? Can't I call just to say hi?"

"Well, yeah. But you usually text if you want to say hi or just come and see me."

"Okay, well, actually, I had a question."

"I knew it. Okay, shoot."

"One of my friends has been really upset with me lately. She says I've been annoying and keeps canceling on me when we have plans, and I've been trying to think if I did something to make her mad, but the only thing I can think of is just texting her when she maybe doesn't want to talk."

"Is this Elise?"

"... No?"

"You have one friend."

"Okay, yeah, it's Elise."

"What's going on? You guys never fight."

"I know! And that's the whole point. I don't know what's wrong because she won't talk to me, you know."

"Hmm. Well, maybe she's going through a hard time. Is she struggling with school? Or fighting with her parents?"

"Maybe? Maybe, she hasn't been going to class at all lately, and I kinda thought she just didn't care, but maybe it's that she's not doing well and is embarrassed. I didn't think about that. And she could be fighting with her parents; they've been home a lot lately."

"Wait, really?"

"Yeah, they spent all of last week home."

"Huh."

"What?"

"It's nothing, I mean, I just haven't seen her Dad at the office for almost two months. I thought he was still in Mexico at the office there."

April 14

I barged into Elise's house without knocking. She was sitting on the couch watching TV. The room was disgusting. She had none of the lights on so everything had that horrible TV glow on it. The floor was covered with dirty clothes and empty takeout boxes and plastic water bottles. I had thought it was bad the last time I was here, but this was terrible.

"I—what—hey."

"Are your parents even here?"

"What?"

"Are. Your. Parents. Here? Or have you been lying to me? My dad said he hasn't seen your dad at the office for two months."

"You asked your dad if I was lying."

"No! Of course not! I was worried that I had done something to make you mad at me and it got brought up!"

"What—why would I be mad at you?"

"You've been avoiding me for weeks! Not responding to my texts, canceling on me every other day, using your parents as an excuse for why you can't see me. What was I supposed to think?"

"Not that I was mad at you! You've got to know, I could never, ever be mad at you. I love you!"

"Well, good! But now I'm mad at you!"

"You're what?"

"I'm mad!"

"At me?"

"Yes!"

"No, you're not."

"Yes, I am! You lied to me. You've been mean."

"You can't be mad at me. You're not—you're never mad at me. You love me."

"I do, but I'm also mad at you. They're not mutually exclusive things you know."

This whole time she had been sitting on the couch – almost like she was too afraid to come near me, but at this, she scrambled up and tried to come over to me, but she tripped over a mound of clothes, so she just stayed on the floor at my feet.

"No, wait. You can't be mad at me."

"You keep saying that, but it doesn't make it true."

"You weren't supposed to be mad! That's not what was supposed to happen!"

"What did you think was going to happen?"

"You were supposed to be happy you didn't have to deal with me anymore!"

"I—Elise, what are you talking about?"

"I've been such a terrible friend. And I just thought it would be easier if I wasn't around as much."

"It would be easier? What are you talking about? I love you, I don't care if you've been a bad friend, I'm worried about you!"

"No, you're not supposed to worry about me."

"I don't care what I'm 'supposed' to do. I love you and I'm worried about you. It's what you do when you love someone, you worry about them."

"Oh god. I'm so sorry. I'm so sorry. Please don't be mad. I love you so much. I'll die if you're mad. You can't be mad.

Don't—don't be mad. I love you. Please—"

"Hey, what—"

"I'm sorry. I'm sorry. I'm—"

"Elise, stop."

"I can't! I didn't mean for any of this to happen."

I dropped to my knees next to her and drew her into a hug. "It's okay. It's going to be okay."

"It's not. It's not." She started to sob.

"We'll figure it out. You and me. Okay?"

"We can't. You can't."

"I can. Do you want to know why? Because I love you. I love you and we're going to figure it out. All right? You don't get a choice. It's you and me, remember? Forever."

April 17

Elise spent the night at my dorm on Friday. I didn't want to leave her alone and I wasn't about to stay in that mess so she came to my room. But she left before I woke up. I waited all weekend, but she never came back.

April 19

I can't believe this shit! I saw Elise leaving one of her classes today. She hasn't been to class in weeks. And I haven't seen her since Friday. And the professor looked happy to see her. She gave Elise a hug when Elise left. This is unbelievable.

## April 21

Elise hasn't texted me in an entire week. I called her this morning because I'm not even mad anymore. I'm just worried. I haven't seen her since Thursday. She didn't answer. Is it me? Did I do something? I don't understand. She was so worried I was going to be mad at her and then she goes and pulls something like this. What am I supposed to do? She doesn't answer my texts. She doesn't come when we make plans. She doesn't want me to come to her house, she actively lies to make sure I stay away. I'm really worried about her.

April 23

Elise finally texted me just to say she was fine and that she would see me later this week. And then she wouldn't answer when I texted her or when I called her.
???

April 24

Didn't see Elise today. No response either.

April 25

Didn't see Elise today.

April 26

Saw Elise today!

She wants to come over on Saturday and spend the weekend.

I mean, of course, I'm gonna say yes, but I just don't even know what to say. Why now? Maybe I just shouldn't ask too many questions, and just be happy she wants to see me. Or what if she wants to come over so she can tell me she doesn't want to see me anymore? Oh god. Oh god. Okay. There's no need to go into doomsday mode. I'm happy I get to see her. That's what matters.

April 29

It's either Saturday night or Sunday morning. I can't see the clock, so I have no idea what time it is, and I'm writing this in the dark, so I don't wake Elise up. She was just so happy today. It's like none of the past month even happened. We spent all day together. We even went to the mall this morning! She wouldn't let me pay for anything, and anything I even remotely said I liked or she thought I would look good in, she bought me. It was crazy. And I told her I didn't need all this stuff, but she said I did and it was her money and I couldn't tell her how to spend it. And I can't exactly argue with that, can I? We went to my favorite restaurant for lunch and watched Indiana Jones mostly just to ogle Harrison Ford and then we ordered pizza for supper. It was like honestly the perfect day. I think she was trying to make up for this past month. How do I tell her that she doesn't need to make up for anything, I'm just glad she's feeling okay.

## April 30

"Here. I got you something."
"What?"
"Here."
"What is it?"
"Open it, dumbass, and then you'll see."
"All right, okay, jeez."
"Mhm."
"Oh my god."
"Do you like it?"
"Oh my god."
"Do you like it?"
"I—Elise, is this a pearl necklace?"
"Yeah."
"This. I—what—this is too much!"
"No, it's not. Come here, let me put it on you."
"It's too much."
"It's perfect. It looks beautiful on you."
"It's too much!"
"No. It's exactly right. You deserve to have beautiful things."
"But—"
"No buts. I wanted to give it to you. So you remember."
"Remember what?"
"The beach."
"Oh, Elise. How could I forget?"

"Just in case."

"I—thank you."

"Don't thank me."

"But—"

"No. I want to thank you."

"What for?"

"For letting me love you."

"Elise."

"You mean more to me than you could possibly know. And I'll never, ever take that for granted."

"Oh."

"I want you to know that I'll love you for the rest of my life."

April 31

Elise left before I woke up this morning. It's still really early. Not even six yet. Why did she leave? Did I do something wrong? I thought we had such a great—

Jesus my phone won't stop ringing. Why are people calling me at six in the morning?

Anyway—

Oh shit, a missed call from my dad? I have to go, call him back.

Elise's mom is calling me?

# May

# June

# July

# August

August 7

My therapist said that sometimes it's easier to write about things than it is to talk about them. I think that's bullshit. But going to therapy was the deal I made with my dad in order to go back to school. So here we are.

"I understand that you used to keep a journal."

"So?"

My therapist's name is Amanda. She wants us to be friends. I think she's crazy.

"There's nothing wrong with keeping a journal. In fact, I actively encourage it for many of my clients."

"Okay."

"Sometimes, it can be hard to find the words to describe what you are feeling out loud. I find that writing about them can help you translate what's in your head into emotions."

"Right."

"I want you to write about what happened last spring."

"Not wanting to talk about it does not mean I want to write about it."

"Your father wants to see that you are making real progress before he decides to send you back to school. In order for me to tell your father you are making progress, I need to see that you want to make progress. Starting a journal will show me that."

August 8

I showed my therapist my journal entry from yesterday. She said it was a start. Whatever the hell that's supposed to mean.

"Starting it is just the first step. If writing about our conversations will help you work up to writing about this spring, then I'm okay with that."

"It doesn't matter if you're okay with it, it's my journal, I can write about whatever I want."

"You are absolutely correct."

She gave me one of those dumb smiles that means she thinks I've done well or whatever.

August 9

I've been meeting with my therapist every day since the first day of August. I don't know if that's like protocol. Or whatever. But I want to go back to school. I can't stay at home anymore. I honestly can't.

"You might find it easier to write it like a conversation."

"What?"

"Your journal."

"I've been writing it. I showed you."

"I know you have. And I'm immensely proud of you. I'm just trying to get you to the next step."

"Whatever."

"As I was saying, sometimes it helps to write as though you are talking to someone. Some people like to write letters to the person."

"Good for them."

"I understand you still haven't read the letter she left you."

"You know I haven't."

"Why don't you write one to her? Tell her all the things you wished you could've told her?"

"If I write one, will you leave me alone?"

"You know I can't. But I will tell your father you're trying."

Dear Elise,

This is stupid. It's not going to work. I have nothing to say to you. And even if I did, what does it matter? You're dead. You can't hear me. That's like the whole point, isn't it?

That's what you wanted? I still don't know what you wanted.

They're worried I'm going to kill myself.

I keep telling them not to worry. That I'm not going to do it. I'm not going to do what you did. I'm not going to take the coward's way out.

'Cause that's what it was, wasn't it? You acted like a coward. You couldn't face it, so you decided to give up. On everything. On *me*.

I still don't get that either.

How you could've left me.

You wanted me to know how much you loved me.

How come you didn't love me enough to stay?

Your mom called me.

Your mom called *me*. I was so confused. I thought someone was dead. I mean I was right about that, I just never in a million years would've thought it was you.

"What's going on?"

"Oh, honey."

"Dad?" He wrapped his arms around me. It was warm that

morning, I didn't need a coat, but my dad was always so worried about me being cold.

"Oh god, honey, I'm so sorry."

"Sorry about what? What's going on? Elise's mom called me, she just said to meet her outside."

"I know, there's something I need to tell you."

I noticed the police first. Sometimes, I wonder if I would've reacted differently if I hadn't noticed them.

"Wait, what's that?"

I pushed past him and started pushing my way through the crowd of people. Towards the science center. Towards the goddamn science center. You always did have some sick sort of irony.

"Honey, wait."

"What's—"

The first thing I noticed was the blood. There was so much of it. Too much of it. It made me sick to my stomach. The next thing I noticed was you. Then I didn't notice anything for a while.

"Honey, are you okay?"

"I'm so sorry. I had no idea…"

"Did you know she was…"

"I should've noticed when she called me the…"

Everyone had something to say. They wanted to know if I knew. If I knew, like you would've told me. That would've ruined it, wouldn't it have? You must've had a big plan. Your mom said you had called them before, and at the time she didn't realize it, but you were saying goodbye. You did all the rounds. You apologized to your teachers.

Then you said goodbye to me. Was it hard? Did you know how you wanted to do it? Should I be honored you wanted to spend your last night with me? What a joke.

I wasn't ready to say goodbye to you.

"We need to get to the hospital."

"What?"

"We need to go to the hospital, Dad, we need to see Elise."

"No, honey."

"Dad, we need to go to the hospital."

"Honey."

"We have to go!"

"Stop."

"We need to go! Why is no one listening to me?"

"Stop, you need to stop. She's not at the hospital. You know that."

"She's—what? Yes, she is."

"No, she's not. She's not at the hospital. She's dead."

I didn't talk to him for a few days after that. How dare he, you know? Of course, I knew you were dead. Logically, but emotionally, that was a whole other story.

"You need to get changed. We have to leave soon."

"I'm not going."

"Don't be ridiculous. You have to go."

"I'm not going."

"I know you don't have a black dress, Elise's mom picked one up for you. You should say thank you when you see her."

"No! I'm not going to thank her because I'm not going to see her."

"Stop it. You have to go. Elise's mom is giving a speech."

"Why is she doing it? She doesn't even know Elise."

"You don't mean that."

"Yes. I do! She can't give the speech, it's her fault Elise is dead!"

Obviously, they made me go.

It was the worst day of my entire life. Worse than the day you died.

I had to look at your body in the casket. They put you in that yellow dress you hated, the one that clashed with your hair. A part of me was happy you would've hated it.

I had to sit there and listen to your mom give the eulogy. She talked about how much life you still had left to live. And how she wished you would've told her what you were going through. And how she knew you would've made an incredible lawyer and had a lovely family someday.

What bullshit.

You didn't want any of that.

You wanted to drop out of school and move to Greece and live on the beach and be with me. Not get married and go to law school.

Sometimes, I wonder what would've happened if I had said yes that day. If everything would've been different, I would've done it. You know, if I had known. I would've said yes in a heartbeat. Anything for you to stay with me.

Your parents moved to Mexico after the funeral. They packed up the house, sold it, and left town within a week. Fitting, don't you think?

I moved back in with my dad.

I didn't do much. For a while.

I was, honestly, the worst to live with.

My dad said it was like living with a ghost. It's why he made me go to therapy.

I stayed in my room all day.

My dad tried to drag me out at first, to get me to eat, to get me to talk, to get me to do something. But I just screamed at him. I feel bad about it now. I should apologize.

I called your mom. Which is, like, incredibly embarrassing. But after I found out they ditched to Mexico, I called her.

"Hello?"

"Why did you leave?"

"Excuse me?"

"Why?"

"I don't think that's an appropriate question for you to ask me."

"And I don't think it's appropriate for you to leave your daughter's grave while the dirt's still settling. Get over it. Now, why did you leave?"

Obviously, that did not work out for me.

She changed her number, and my dad narrowly convinced her out of getting a restraining order on me. Which I think was a little over dramatic considering the fact she was in Mexico and 40, but whatever. I'm glad she's scared of me.

I was mad for a long time.

Mad at your mom for abandoning you. Mad at myself for not figuring it out. Mad at my dad for talking to me. Mad at the girl who killed herself in January for giving you the idea. Mad at you.

I was worried that once I stopped feeling mad, I wouldn't feel anything anymore. I didn't realize I had already stopped. I wonder if that's what you were feeling when you did it. That nothingness. The loneliness. The despair. Probably.

But here's what I don't get.

You were sick.

I know that.

Everyone tells me that.

There was something wrong with your brain. You needed help.

But I would've helped you.

You have to know I would've.

I would've given you the whole world if you had only asked.

Why didn't you ask?

Why didn't you tell me?

We could've had a future. We could've had everything you wanted. Greece. The beach. Happiness.

I love you.

I know you loved me.

That much I know.

But maybe you didn't love me like I love you.

Because, I never.

I never would've left you.

Not when you needed me. Not when you didn't.

You couldn't have forced me to go.

How could you say you loved me when you didn't love me enough to stay?

*Promise me you'll read this letter. If I know you at all, you won't want to, but please do. I know you'll be mad. And I'm sorry. God, I'm so sorry. I know you'll never forgive me, and that's okay. I'll never forgive myself either.*

*It's okay for you to be mad. It's okay for you to be horribly furious at me. Know that I don't blame you for being mad. Please be mad at me. Don't be mad at yourself.*

*I could've told you. I had every opportunity to. I almost did a hundred times. I really almost did the day you broke into my house because you thought I had died. And isn't that ironic? But I never would've disappeared without saying goodbye. It's not that I didn't trust you. I trusted you more than I trusted myself. I don't have a good explanation for why I didn't tell you. At least not one you'll want to hear.*

*But the truth is, is that your life will be better without me in it. I knew it for certain the first time you were angry with me. You had never been angry with me before that, and I was shocked. I never imagined that you would be angry with me for isolating myself. Hurt, yes. But never angry.*

*I never wanted it to be like this. I wanted to disappear from your life, slow enough that you'd forget about me before I was gone. But you wouldn't let me. You're stubborn like that. That's one of the things I love about you. You texted me every day, called, and showed up at my house. You wouldn't let me disappear.*

*You always knew what you wanted.*
*I'm honored that at one time it was me.*
*Do you wear the necklace I gave you?*
*I hope you do.*

*That week we spent on the beach was the happiest I ever remember being. If there is an afterlife, I know that that will be mine. You looked so beautiful on the sand, so happy just to be out in the sun. I would've given you the world. I almost asked you to marry me.*

*I don't think you understood how much I loved you. But that's okay. My love does not have conditions. I'm sorry if I made it seem like it did. I would've loved you even if you didn't want to move halfway across the world and pledge yourself to a life of not getting married to anyone but me. I would've loved you if you didn't love me at all. But I'm so grateful you did.*

*Promise me you'll finish school.*

*It was important to you at one point, and even if it's not important to you now, it's still important to you. Please do it for me?*

*I want you to be able to do whatever it is you want to in this world.*

*I want you to be happy and have a good life and find someone who loves you the way you are meant to be loved.*

*I want you to not have to worry about me anymore.*
*Because that's what love is to you, isn't it?*
*Worrying about someone.*
*Wondering if they're eating enough, sleeping too much.*
*Don't worry about me anymore.*

*If you think of me, think of me that day on the beach. The day we swam under the stars, and you told me you'd move to Greece with me.*

*That's how I want to remember you.*
*I want that to be how you remember me.*
*I love you.*
*Now and forever.*
*Goodbye.*

*With Love,*
*Elise*